ARD

BEEZY AT BAT

by Megan McDonald

illustrated by Nancy Poydar

ORCHARD BOOKS • NEW YORK

Orchard Books, 95 Madison Avenue, New York, NY 10016

Manufactured in the United States of America
Printed by Barton Press, Inc. Bound by Horowitz/Rae
Book design by Mina Greenstein
The text of this book is set in 20 point Stempel Garamond.
The illustrations are gouache paintings reproduced in full color.
10 9 8 7 6 5 4 3 2 1

Library of Congress Cataloging-in-Publication Data
McDonald, Megan. Beezy at bat / by Megan McDonald ;
illustrated by Nancy Poydar. 1st American ed. p. cm.
Summary: Three stories in which Beezy cracks nuts and riddles, picks berries,
and plays baseball.
ISBN 0-531-30085-4 (tr. : alk. paper). — ISBN 0-531-33085-0 (lib. ed. : alk. paper)
[1. Grandmothers—Fiction. 2. Friendship—Fiction. 3. Florida—Fiction.]
I. Poydar, Nancy, ill. II. Title.
PZ7.M478419Bg 1998 [E]—dc21 97-35015

For Louise, Annie, and Eliza
—M.M.

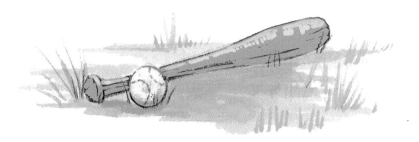

Contents

Cracking Riddles

Gran sat in her rocker.

Beezy sat on the porch steps.

Funnybone curled up at Gran's feet.

The sun started down.

The corn looked like gold in the light.

"Hey, Ruby. Hey, Beezy,"
said Mr. Gumm.
Ruby was Gran.
Beezy was Beezy.
"Pull up a chair, Gumm," said Gran.
Gumm was Mr. Gumm.

"See these nuts?" asked Beezy.

"I see two nuts
sitting on the porch," Mr. Gumm said.

"Funny, funny," said Beezy.

"Help us crack nuts, Mr. Gumm.
Shells go here."

Mr. Gumm pretended

to crack a nut with his teeth.

"Not with your teeth, Mr. Gumm!"

"I was just fooling you, Beezy.

Did you know, you can't crack nuts

without cracking riddles?"

Mr. Gumm said.

"Tell me a riddle, Mr. Gumm."

"What stands up

but never sits down?"

Beezy looked up at the sky.

Beezy looked down at the ground.

"I give up."

"A tree," said Mr. Gumm.

Gran had a riddle.

"What is as light as a feather,

but no one wants to carry it?"

"A leaf?" Beezy asked.

"Dust?" asked Mr. Gumm.

"What?" Beezy asked.

"A mosquito, that's what," Gran said.

"Here's one for you, Beezy.

What does a bat need after a bath?

Give up?

A bat mat!"

"My turn," said Beezy.

"What has ears but can't hear?"

"Corn?" asked Mr. Gumm.

"No," said Beezy.

"Merlin when he had a bee

in his ear!"

It was dark out now.

"This sure was fun," said Mr. Gumm.

"We did not crack many nuts,"
Gran said.

"But we sure did crack
a whole lot of riddles!"

Trouble

"Let's pick blackberries," said Beezy.

"Let's not and say we did," Merlin said.

Beezy asked, "Why?"

"Snakes," said Merlin.

"Don't be silly," said Beezy.

Beezy hooked a tin can to her belt.

"Watch out for snakes!" Gran called.

Merlin picked up a stick.

A special snake stick.

Just in case.

They ran down to the creek.

Merlin wanted to catch minnows.

Merlin wanted to skip stones.

Merlin wanted to sail leaf boats.

Anything but snakes.

Plunk. Beezy dropped a berry
in her can.

Plunk. Plunk. Plunk.

"Let's go home now,"
Merlin said.
"Merlin, you only
picked three berries."

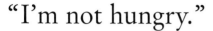

"I'm not hungry."
Beezy ate three berries.
Beezy ate three more berries.

Juice ran down her chin.
Juice ran down her arm.
Juice ran down her leg,
inside her sock!

She licked her arm.

She licked her chin.

She licked her leg!

Juice stained her teeth purple.
Juice stained her shirt purple
in the shape of Florida!

SSSSSSS! Merlin heard a snake.

He held out his snake stick.

Beezy said it was the wind.

SSSSSSS! Merlin heard a snake again.

Beezy stood on tiptoe.

She reached in the

blackberry bushes.

SSSSSSS!

A snake!

Beezy picked up the snake.

Merlin ran.

He dropped his special snake stick.

Beezy ran after him.

"Gran," Beezy called.

Gran was planting seeds
in the garden.

"Guess what we found," said Beezy.

"I hope you did not
bring home a snake," Gran said.

"You know what I say about snakes.
Never trouble trouble
till trouble troubles you."
Beezy had to hide the snake. Fast.
She saw Gran's old shirt
hanging on the fence post.
The shirt had two big pockets.
Perfect!

Gran turned around.

"Blackberries!" said Gran.

"And here I was

thinking you found a snake.

Merlin, would you like to stay

and make ice cream?

Let's see if we can find

the ice cream maker."

Gran picked up the tools.

Gran picked up her shirt.

She tied the shirt around her waist.

"I have to go," said Merlin.

"So soon?" asked Gran.

"Yes," said Merlin.

"Gran?" said Beezy.

"Your shirt is in trouble."

"My shirt?"

"Yes," said Beezy.

"I have to put the trouble back

before it troubles you."

Gran gave Beezy the old shirt.

Merlin ran.

"Wait for me," said Beezy.

Gran called,

"When you are out of trouble,

come back for some ice cream."

Jaws

Play ball!

The Hurricanes were playing the Jets.

Beezy asked, "Where's Jordan?

We need one more player."

Sarafina rode past on her unicycle.

"Hurry up," said the Jets.

"We want to play ball."

Sarafina rode past again.

"Let's ask Sarafina Zippy,"
said Merlin.

"She's too short," said Lucy.

Ben said, "She doesn't even have
a mitt."

"Meet Jaws," Sarafina said.

Her mitt had a shark face on it.

"Did you draw that?" Merlin asked.

Sarafina said, "I can draw
stingrays too."

"Do you want to play or not?"
called the Jets.

"Batter up," said Beezy.

The Hurricanes were up first.

Beezy hit the ball.

Merlin hit the ball.

Lucy and Ben hit the ball.

Sarafina Zippy was up.

She closed her eyes.

Strike one!

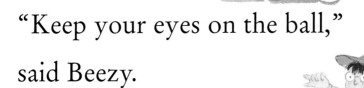

"Keep your eyes on the ball,"

said Beezy.

The pitcher threw the ball.

Sarafina jumped out of the way.

Strike two!

Merlin said, "Keep your bat
in the air."

The next pitch hit Sarafina's bat.

It landed in the catcher's mitt.

"Out!" yelled the Jets.

"She forgot to swing!" Ben cried.

"Don't you play baseball

in the circus?" Lucy yelled.

"Don't mind them," said Beezy

and Merlin.

Sarafina played right field.

Lester was up.

Lester was Home Run King
for the Jets.

Lester had a plan.

Smack! He hit the ball.

The ball sailed over Sarafina's head.

She did not move.

The ball hit the fence.

Home run for the Jets!

"I'll be ready for you

next time,"

Sarafina said.

Next time, Lester sent the ball
to right field again.

Sarafina ran.

She chased the ball

with her shark mitt.

Not fast enough!

Another home run!

"Just you wait, Lester," said Sarafina.

"You can't outsmart the shark."

Bottom of the ninth.

Lester was up again.

Bases were loaded. Two outs.

The score was tied, six to six.

Lester stepped up to the plate.

He spit on his hands.

He rubbed spit on the bat.

"Les-ter! Les-ter!" chanted the Jets.
"Wish me luck, Jaws," Sarafina said.
She had a plan. She closed her eyes.
She wished on her
alligator-tooth necklace.

Lester hit the ball.

The ball went up, up, up.

A pop fly over right field.

So high it looked like a bird.

Sarafina jumped on her unicycle.

She rode backward, eyes on the ball.

She stood up on the pedals.

She held Jaws high.

She held Jaws open.

Bam!

The ball landed in her mitt.

Sarafina fell off her unicycle

with a crash.

She clamped down on that ball

with shark's teeth.

"OUT!" shouted the Hurricanes.

"Wow," said the Jets.

"Wow," said the Hurricanes.

"Who is that girl?" the Jets asked.

"Sarafina Zippy," said the Hurricanes.

"Can she play ball!"

"And she knows magic tricks,"
Merlin said.

"And she can jump two ropes,"
said Beezy.

"Are you really from the circus?"

"Is your tattoo a lightning bolt?"

"Let's see that shark mitt."

"Can you draw a stingray on mine?"

"After the game,"
Sarafina told them.

"Tenth inning.

I'm up."